The Real, True
DULCIE CAMPBELL

Cynthia DeFelice

PICTURES BY **R. W. Alley**

New Hanover County Public Library
201 Chestnut Street
Wilmington, NC 28401

Farrar, Straus and Giroux / New York

One Saturday afternoon, when Dulcie Campbell was doing her chores, it occurred to her that a terrible mistake had been made on the day she was born.

Someone—a careless nurse or a daydreaming doctor or, more likely, a wicked fairy—must have taken her from her satin-lined, jewel-encrusted royal crib and placed her in the quite ordinary crib of another, quite ordinary baby.

And in that way, the extraordinary Princess Dulcinea (for that, she knew, was her real, true name) ended up living with a quite ordinary family on a quite ordinary farm in the quite ordinary town of Hollyhock, Iowa, mucking out the chicken coop.

There was a woman who lived in the house, but she was no queen.

"My *real* mother has hundreds of servants who do all the work, and she never makes me set the table. My real mother buys me silken gowns, and doesn't even own a sewing machine. My real mother lets me eat chocolates all day long and does not believe in broccoli. She never wears worn-out old bunny slippers with missing ears."

There was a man who lived in the house, too, but he was no king.

"My *real* father lets me watch TV as late as I want, and never wakes me up in the morning to help with the milking. My real father had a throne built just for me, and he's never even heard of a time-out chair. My real father has a long, soft, flowing beard, not scratchy whiskers, and he does not have manure stuck to his boots."

There was a boy who slept in the room next to hers, but he was no prince.

"My *real* brother is handsome and charming. He does not have bunchy red hair and missing teeth and freckles. My real brother has so many toys of his own that he never messes with mine. My real brother does not steal my underpants and wear them on his head."

Even Ralph was not Dulcie's real dog.

"My *real* dog would never roll around on a dead woodchuck. My real dog doesn't have dog breath. My real dog doesn't sniff people in embarrassing places."

"I must inform you that I am really a princess," she announced
to the people in the house.

"Well now, I've always known you were something special,
sweet pea," said the man.

"A princess," said the woman. "Can you imagine that!"

"Not really," said the boy.

"Furthermore," Dulcie continued grandly, "I command you
to call me by my real, true name, Princess Dulcinea."
"Of course, Your Highness," said the man.
"Certainly, Princess Dulcinea," said the woman.
"Fat chance," said the boy.

"I must go now to live the life I was born for," said Dulcie.

"Goodbye," said the woman.

"Good luck," said the man.

"Good riddance," said the boy.

"Farewell," called Dulcie.

"Take a warm jacket!" called the woman.

"Don't forget your book!" called the man.

"I thought you said you were leaving!" shouted the boy.

Closing the door behind her, Dulcie set off into the wide world to find her rightful place.

Everywhere she went, she was recognized by one and all as the princess she truly was.

Her admiring subjects bowed and bobbed and curtsied.

They ooohed.

They aaahed.

They groveled adoringly at her feet.

They lined the fences, murmuring in awe at the sight of her.

They scurried forward to trumpet her praises.

Soon Dulcie saw the towers of a great palace. She went inside and sat on a throne to wait for her real, true family to appear. To help pass the time, she opened her book of fairy tales and began to read.

The book was full of stories about princesses.

The first princess wore beautiful silken gowns, married a prince, and lived happily ever after. Dulcie smiled and eagerly read on.

The next princess was left by her father with a wicked queen who made her wear rags and sleep in the ashes. Dulcie's smile began to fade.

A wicked fairy placed a spell on another princess, who slept for a hundred years.

One princess was imprisoned in the palace of the West Wind, one was locked in a tower by a witch, one was turned to stone, and one had to keep house for an ogre.

One even had to kiss a frog.

"Blech," said Dulcie, snapping the book shut.

It was all very disappointing. She had thought the life of a princess would be perfect, but instead it sounded boring and hard and downright yucky.

She looked down at the clothes her mother had made for her. They weren't made of silk, but they weren't rags, either.

Her father made her clean up after chickens, but they weren't nearly as grody as ogres.

Her parents made her go to bed when she wasn't even tired, but not for a hundred years, and never in the ashes. Once in a while they sent her to the time-out chair, but she knew they would never, ever lock her in a tower.

The life of a princess seemed lonely. Dulcie was beginning to feel lonely, too. Right at that moment, there was nothing she wanted to see more than her real, true mother's worn-out old bunny slippers, and nothing she'd rather feel than her real, true father's scratchy whiskers, and nothing she'd rather smell than the soft, warm fur on the neck of her real, true dog, Ralph. She thought it might even be nice to see her brother.

Dulcie got up to leave and noticed that it had grown quite dark. She peered uneasily into the deep, black shadows. There, in a cobwebby corner, hid a terrible troll. Along the wall, witches and wicked fairies watched and whispered. Ogres ogled from overhead.

To Dulcie's dismay, she found she was under their spell. She felt as if she'd been turned to stone.

"Hey!" she cried out. "There's been a mistake. I'm no princess."

Titters and giggles came from the corners.

"I'd rather eat broccoli than kiss a frog any day!" she called.

Still the voices muttered and mocked her.

"You need proof that I'm not a princess? Take a look at my brother!"

The creatures lurked and laughed and licked their lips.

Dulcie swallowed hard. Tears were beginning to prickle in her eyes when she remembered something. "Wait a second," she said. "If I'm not a princess, which I really, truly am *not*, then you guys aren't real, true trolls and ogres and witches and wicked fairies, either! So could you please go away now?"

Dulcie closed her eyes.

When she opened them again, she was relieved to see shovels and pitchforks, not witches and wicked fairies, lining the walls. Instead of ogres, milk pails and rolls of baling wire filled the hayloft. In the corner stood a tractor, not a troll. She was in her own, true barn on her own, true farm.

Far away a voice was calling, "*Dul-cee!* Dulcie Campbell!"

Faster than the West Wind, Dulcie ran out to the barnyard. She flew toward the sound of her real, true name.

Soon she was lifted high in the air. She felt the scratch of whiskers on her cheek and breathed in the rich, familiar smell of her real, true father.

"Mmm, mmm," he said, squeezing her tight. "You feel mighty good, Princess."

"It's just me, Dad. Dulcie Campbell."

"Why, so it is."

They walked toward the glow shining from the windows of Dulcie's real, true home.

Inside, Dulcie's real, true dog, Ralph, sniffed her all over and licked her face and thumped his tail with joy.

Her real, true mother called from the kitchen, "Is that you, Dulcie? Thank goodness! Come help me set the table for supper."

Her real, true brother muttered, "I knew it was too good to last."

Dulcie Campbell and her real, true family sat down to a feast fit for a princess.

For my real, true sister, Corky —C.D.

For Zoë —R.W. A.

Text copyright © 2002 by Cynthia C. DeFelice
Pictures copyright © 2002 by R. W. Alley
All rights reserved
Distributed in Canada by Douglas & McIntyre Ltd.
Color separations by Hong Kong Scanner Arts
Printed and bound in the United States of America by Berryville Graphics
Typography by Robbin Gourley
First edition, 2002
1 3 5 7 9 10 8 6 4 2

Library of Congress Cataloging-in-Publication Data
DeFelice, Cynthia C.
The real, true Dulcie Campbell / Cynthia DeFelice ; pictures by R. W. Alley.— 1st ed.
        p. cm.
        Summary: Believing she is a princess, Dulcie Campbell leaves home to seek her true family, but she finds
by reading a book of fairy tales that being a princess is not what she thought.
        ISBN 0-374-36220-3
        [1. Family—Fiction.   2. Princesses—Fiction.   3. Books and reading—Fiction.]   I. Alley, R. W. (Robert W.), ill.   II. Title.

PZ7.D3597 Re 2002
[E]—dc21

                                                                                                        00-58736